Date Due

DEC 2 2 97			
FEB 0 5 '98			
MAR 1 6 '98			
APR 1 6 '98			
AUG 3 1 '98			
NOV 0 6 '98			
AUG 1 2 '02			
AUG 8 02			
MAR 2 4 03			
JUN 0 4 03			

11/97

Jackson
Coun

Services

HEADQUARTERS
413 W.Main
Medford, Oregon 97501

The Gratitude of Kings

MARION ZIMMER BRADLEY

The Gratitude *of* Kings

A ROC BOOK

ROC
Published by the Penguin Group
Penguin Putnam Inc., 375 Hudson Street,
New York, New York 10014, U.S.A.
Penguin Books Ltd, 27 Wrights Lane, London W8 5TZ, England
Penguin Books Australia Ltd, Ringwood, Victoria, Australia
Penguin Books Canada Ltd, 10 Alcorn Avenue,
Toronto, Ontario, Canada M4V 3B2
Penguin Books (N.Z.) Ltd, 182–190 Wairau Road,
Auckland 10, New Zealand

Penguin Books Ltd, Registered Offices:
Harmondsworth, Middlesex, England

First published by Roc, an imprint of Dutton Signet,
a member of Penguin Putnam Inc.
Published by arrangement with The Wildside Press.
For information address The Wildside
Press, 522 Park Avenue, Berkeley Heights, New Jersey 07922.

First Printing, December, 1997
1   3   5   7   9   10   8   6   4   2

 REGISTERED TRADEMARK—MARCA REGISTRADA

LIBRARY OF CONGRESS CATALOGING-IN-PUBLICATION DATA:
Bradley, Marion Zimmer.
The gratitude of kings / Marion Zimmer Bradley.
p.   cm.
ISBN 0-451-45641-6
I. Title.
PS3552.R228G69   1997
813'.54—dc21   97-17720
                                                          CIP

Printed in the United States of America
Set in Garamond
Designed by Jesse Cohen

For my daughter, Moira,
and my grandson, Robert Jeffrey

LYTHANDE, ADEPT OF the Blue Star, mercenary magician and sometime minstrel, entered the inner courtyard of the royal castle of Tschardain still accompanied by four guards. Twelve more had split off from the traveling party in the outer courtyard. It had been quite an escort for one solitary magician, who needed no guards at all for safety, but Lythande knew that their master liked to make showy gestures, especially if other people were doing the work involved. No doubt he was thrilled to be able to send out such a large party of men to escort one magician. He was not motivated by chivalry; the fact that she was a woman was Lythande's deepest secret, the one that guarded her magical powers. Lythande had, on a few occasions, even killed to keep that secret. If she were proclaimed a woman in the hearing of any man, the Power of the Blue Star would be gone from her and she would die.

In truth, Lythande was not entirely sure that she wished to be here. The guard captain sent to summon her had informed her that his master, Lord Tashgan, would be most grateful if the magician would accept this invitation to his coronation, and Lythande, in her many centuries of life, was not without experience in the "gratitude" of kings. She had dealt briefly with Tashgan about ten years before, when his two elder brothers died and left him as his father's sole heir. Then he had been Tashgan the wandering minstrel, who traveled each year from his father's court to Northwander and back, drinking and womanizing the entire way. His travels had not been entirely voluntary; a spell on his lute, set by the court magician at his brothers' request, enforced his route and the duration of his stay in each town and city. They had made certain that he could not remain in one place long enough to gather allies who would plot against them, but when their deaths made him his father's heir the spell had become a real problem. Lythande had traded lutes with him, enabling him to go home to the kingdom he was to inherit; and, so far as she knew, he had been content with that solution.

Lythande was curious to see what settling down had done to Tashgan. The guards told her only that his father had died at long last and that Tashgan required her services. And it was certainly more pleasant to travel with other people who were doing the hard work at campsites and paying the reckoning at the inns.

The journey into the mountains of Tschardain was a surprisingly easy one. The biggest problem was that a couple of the guards seemed terrified of Lythande—or perhaps merely of magicians in general. The weather was mild for early winter, the inns were comfortable and close enough together for a leisurely journey, and the roads were well maintained. Nevertheless Lythande was surprised to see, as they approached the castle, what appeared to be a respectable-size fair being set up in a flat expanse of rock below the castle walls. She started to ask the guards about it, but the captain said hastily that it was just the trade fair, they did it every year, it wouldn't start until the morrow, it was nothing to concern the master magician, and Lord Tashgan was waiting, so if it would please the honorable magician to accompany them . . . Lythande suspected that the poor man would have dragged her into the castle by the hair, if he had only dared.

The inner courtyard was full of people hard at work, preparing for Tashgan's coronation as High King of Tschardain. The noise was incredible, the air was full of smoke and dust—and a sudden streak of cobalt-blue fire. The guard on Lythande's left, a young man who had been nervous the entire trip, gasped and ducked as the fire passed right over his head and straight toward Lythande's shoulder.

Even though her cloak was fireproof, Lythande disliked having to twist her head to speak to anything on her shoulder; it was such an awkward angle. Murmuring a spell to fireproof her skin, she calmly put up a hand and the salamander landed on her left wrist, enabling her to hold it in front of her. As she half expected, she recognized the creature. While most people looking at it would see only a ball of flame or, if they looked closely, a miniature dragon with flames licking about its form, Lythande had worked with elementals many times in her long career and could distinguish their differences as well as their similarities.

"Greetings, Essence of Fire," she said gravely. The guards looked startled, and the nervous one shied away, staring wide-eyed at Lythande. Lythande ignored

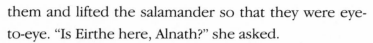

them and lifted the salamander so that they were eye-to-eye. "Is Eirthe here, Alnath?" she asked.

The salamander streaked off through the air again, clearing a path behind it. Lythande followed, ignoring the pair of guards who hurried after her.

The flaming trail led to a roped-off work area at one side of the courtyard. Alnath dove beneath a large cauldron of hot blue wax, into the low fire burning there. The dark-haired woman bending over the cauldron scarcely spared the salamander a glance as she carefully dipped a row of slender candles suspended from a wooden bar into the cauldron, lifted them out, and set them on a rack for the latest coat to dry. Then she looked up, met Lythande's eyes, and smiled.

"Lythande," she said. "So they did find you."

"As you see," Lythande replied. Eirthe Candlemaker had been a friend of hers for more than a decade, and was one of the few women who knew Lythande's secret. Although everyone who had known Lythande before she became an Adept was now long dead, from time to time a woman would discover what she truly was. As long as Lythande could trust the woman not to betray her—and as long as none of Lythande's enemies suspected that the woman knew anything worth torturing her for—Lythande could keep her as a friend. Such friendships were, necessarily, rare, and this was one Lythande particularly valued.

By now Eirthe must be in her mid-thirties, but she still looked like a girl of twenty, except for her hands, which were scarred and burned from years of handling hot wax, fire, and Alnath.

"What brings you here, Eirthe?" Lythande asked. "You are far from home."

"The funeral, the coronation, the wedding, and the trade fair, not necessarily in that order," Eirthe answered briefly, picking up another row of candles and dipping them into the melted wax.

"I saw the fairgrounds on the way in," Lythande said,

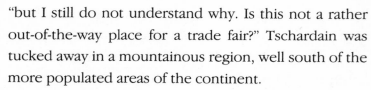

"but I still do not understand why. Is this not a rather out-of-the-way place for a trade fair?" Tschardain was tucked away in a mountainous region, well south of the more populated areas of the continent.

"It's Lord Tashgan's main contribution to the kingdom's economy," Eirthe explained. "He arranged the first one the year after he came back here, inviting many of us from Old Gandrin." She smiled fondly. "I think he missed us, once he no longer came to our fair each spring, so he brought us to him. Some of us remain through Yule-tide as well; Tashgan is a gracious host. I usually stay for a while—it's not as if I had any family left to spend the season with." For an instant Eirthe looked sad, then she seemed to pull her thoughts back to business. "The fair is actually fairly profitable; he holds it the week before the Yule-feast, so everyone is shopping for gifts. There's also a pass through the eastern mountains between Tschardain and Valantia, which is the trade center for everything on their side of the mountains. That's where his bride comes from."

"So Tashgan is marrying. How interesting." Lythande forced her features into a suitably grave expression.

Eirthe didn't even try. She grinned openly. "Well, he does need an heir—he's the last of his family left. You should start thinking of suitable music for the wedding; it will be celebrated a week from today."

"Is *that* why he had me come all this way?" Few things in life truly surprised Lythande after centuries of adventure, but it did seem that Tashgan could have found a minstrel closer to home. In fact, he fancied himself quite a musician—or had when Lythande had seen him last—so surely he must have at least one minstrel at his court. "I suppose I should go present myself to him," she added, "and leave you to your work."

"It is true that I still have a lot to do," Eirthe admitted.

"I always come early for the fair, so I have plenty of time to make candles here instead of having to transport them, but I wasn't counting on the funeral and all the rest." She picked up another row of candles. "I'll see you later."

"*Y*OU ARE WELL come to my court, Master Magician," Tashgan said, smiling broadly. From his voice one would have supposed Lythande to be his oldest and dearest friend.

The Blue Star between Lythande's brows prickled. She had been aware ever since she entered the hall that there was magic at work here. What was it?

Tashgan sat in an elaborately carved wooden chair on a stone dais at the end of the great hall. A fire roared in the hearth behind him in addition to the large fires in the side hearths, so the room felt comfortably warm—or at least as warm as any stone room in a castle could be.

Two women sat with him: the younger an absolutely gorgeous young woman who sat on a slightly less ornate chair to his right. She had long midnight-black hair curling at the ends and sapphire-blue eyes which looked out of a face that could have been carved of marble or alabaster, except for the rose color in her cheeks. Her features were so perfectly symmetrical and regular that she could truthfully be called inhumanly beautiful. She looked like a very well made doll. Lythande's gaze moved to a much older woman who flowed over a stool on the girl's other side. Her heavy body was dressed in concealing dark clothing, and she had thin tight lips and a discontented expression. Lythande felt an instant dislike. Who was she?

Tashgan had been eyeing the leather case on

Lythande's back. "Is that a new lute? You must play for us after dinner."

Lythande bowed silently in assent. She never minded playing; music had been her first love, before she came to know magic, and it was still an important part of her. Besides that, the practice of music held much less potential for disaster than that of magic.

"Certainly music is a much more appropriate profession for a man than magic is," snapped the elderly woman sitting on the dais.

Tashgan smiled again, but with the air of someone trying to be polite while listening once again to an argument he had heard too many times already. "I am sure that Lythande will change your mind about men and magic, Lady," he said. Then he turned to Lythande again. "Permit me to present you to my promised bride, Princess Velvet of Valantia." Lythande bowed to the princess, who nodded a bit stiffly in return. "And this is her lady-in-waiting, Lady Mirwen."

Lythande bowed again, less deeply, but Lady Mirwen simply sniffed and turned away. *Apparently she does not wish the acquaintance,* Lythande thought. *Princess Velvet seems merely shy. How does she come to this marriage? Did Tashgan pick her for her name? He was ever fond of fine fabrics.*

Tashgan continued, turning to Lady Mirwen, "Lythande will be my champion in the Marriage Games."

This produced an outraged gasp. "That is completely impossible! A man cannot work magic—especially in such a delicate matter. Women are the only ones with the proper delicacy of touch and subtlety of feeling."

Subtlety of feeling? Lythande thought with a touch of amusement. *That woman would not know "subtle" if it walked up and introduced itself to her.*

"Lady Mirwen," Tashgan said firmly. "This is my country, not yours. I am willing to conform to your customs so far as to include your rituals in my wedding, but the choice of champion is mine, and I will not be bound by your customs there. I have dealt with female magicians—when I was young, my father's court magician was a woman—and I have dealt with Lythande, and I choose Lythande."

"My lord?" Princess Velvet murmured softly at his side.

Tashgan turned to her with an indulgent smile. "Yes, my lady?"

"What happened to your father's court magician? Did you turn her away when you came to the throne?"

Tashgan shook his head. "No, indeed. Within her abilities, Ellifanwy was extremely skilled at her job. Unfortunately, she chose to venture outside her area of competence. She died in a were-dragon's lair years ago, before I ever came back to court."

"And what did *you* consider her area of competence to be?" Lady Mirwen asked scathingly. "Love spells?" From her tone, she appeared to think there was no reason for her to be even polite to her charge's future husband.

The Blue Star prickled again. This woman had magic, Lythande realized; that much was sure. But something felt dreadfully wrong. This marriage was more—or maybe less—than it seemed.

Tashgan was momentarily speechless, which Lythande felt to be just as well—love spells were *exactly* what he had considered to be the pinnacle of Ellifanwy's work. But Lythande had known Ellifanwy as well, and while the woman had not been in her class—or anywhere near it—she had possessed strong skills in several areas.

"Actually," Lythande said before Tashgan could recover enough to open his mouth and blurt out anything unfortunate, "she was famous for her binding spells. Things she bound *stayed* bound." *Like that lute of Tashgan's.*

"Even beyond her death," Tashgan said, nodding. "Were she still with us, Lady Mirwen, perhaps I would choose her as your opponent, but, alas, she is no longer here. As you seem to doubt a man's abilities in this matter, surely you do not fear to match yourself against Lythande."

"Certainly not!" Mirwen snapped.

"Before I agree to this matter," Lythande said smoothly, "perhaps someone would care to explain just what it involves. 'Marriage Games' could be anything—from animated banquet sweets up to a magical duel to the death, although anything that drastic would doubt-less cast a damper on the festivities."

"Isn't that just like a man," Mirwen said, "always thinking of death."

You inspire such thoughts in me, Lady, Lythande thought wryly, but she said nothing aloud.

Princess Velvet took a deep breath and replied, "They are a contest of skill, Master Magician. The two sorcer-esses—er, sorcerers—vie to see who can create the most fantastic and beautiful illusions." She looked nervously at Lythande and added, "In Valantia, it is generally women who practice this sort of sorcery, but I don't believe anything forbids a man to do so—if he wants to, I mean." She looked nervously at Lady Mirwen and then at Prince Tashgan. He smiled dotingly and reached over to take her hand.

"Have you seen many of these contests, Princess?" Lythande asked.

Velvet nodded. "I have nine older sisters, and I attended all their weddings."

" 'Most fantastic and beautiful,' " Lythande mused aloud. "Who judges these contests?"

"The wedding guests do," Velvet replied. "Everyone except the bride and groom."

"The bride and groom presumably having other things on their minds?" Lythande asked, smiling.

Velvet blushed and looked at her lap. Tashgan chuckled.

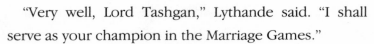

"Very well, Lord Tashgan," Lythande said. "I shall serve as your champion in the Marriage Games."

"Excellent," Tashgan said enthusiastically. "I am most grateful to you. I know that you will make my wedding day a day that will be long remembered in my kingdom."

Somehow I feel certain it will be, Lythande thought, *although it may not be in the way any of us expects. I have an odd feeling about this . . .*

"I shall have my chamberlain escort you to your suite," Tashgan continued, raising a hand to beckon the man forward. "We have put you next to Eirthe Candlemaker—as I recall, you and she are great friends."

From the smirk on his face, he had—and was giving everyone in the room—entirely the wrong idea of what kind of friends Lythande and Eirthe were, but Lythande did not doubt that Eirthe could take care of her own reputation. Besides, she suspected that this was Tashgan's way of telling her that he knew she had stopped to talk to Eirthe before seeing him.

"As your highness says," she replied, bowing, before she turned to follow the chamberlain. She intended to have a long talk with Eirthe in any case; the younger woman could doubtless tell her a good deal about the current situation.

*L*YTHANDE FOUND HER suite luxurious indeed; Tashgan was apparently displaying his gratitude to her with more than mere words. Eirthe's room was next to Lythande's, but the candlemaker was not there, even after dinner when it was dark outside. She frowned thoughtfully and headed to the inner courtyard.

Eirthe was still dipping candles, one rod after another, in a smooth unbroken rhythm. She had obviously melted a new pot of wax; this batch was golden instead of blue. She had plenty of light to work by; eight of Cadmon's goblets, each with a ball of fire inside it, sat in a circle around her.

Cadmon and Eirthe had been partners until Cadmon's death; they had been under curses which canceled each other. Until Eirthe, with some assistance from Lythande, had managed to free herself from her curse, nothing would burn near her, nor could any candles she made. Cadmon had been a glassblower, but anything flammable put in his glass burned up in an instant. Anything that was *not* usually flammable would burn at a normal speed as if it were flammable. Put together, his glassware and Eirthe's candles made excellent lamps.

Alnath's favorite resting place was a piece Cadmon had originally intended as a fishbowl. Any fish put in it would have been broiled to charcoal before it could be dumped out, but it was the perfect home for a salamander. At the moment, however, Alnath lay in the fire under the cauldron, which, Lythande knew, was her normal place when Eirthe was working.

Lythande crossed between two of the goblets, frowning as she felt the faint flicker of a very simple warding spell. "Eirthe, what is going on here?" she demanded.

Eirthe looked up as she switched rods. "If you mean the warding spell, it's to keep people from getting burned. Between the salamanders, the fire, and the wax dripping, this is a dangerous area for the unwary. Tashgan *does* tend to choose his servants for their looks rather than their brains."

"That is true enough," Lythande agreed. Then Eirthe's earlier words registered. "Salamanders?" She took a closer look at the goblets around her. "Sweet Queen of Life, where did they all come from?"

"Alnath had babies last year," Eirthe informed her. "She comes into heat—no pun intended—every six years or so, but last year was the first time there was another salamander around when she did."

"How can you tell that a salamander is in heat?" Lythande asked, genuinely curious. Alnath was the only salamander she had ever spent much time with, and the only thing she had learned on the subject in the course of her magical studies was that salamanders were the elementals associated with fire and were considered capricious and dangerous. Of course, all elementals were considered capricious and dangerous—and so, frequently, were the elements they represented.

Eirthe laughed. "I can feel it through my link with her. It makes me restless and snappish; when she actually mated I didn't dare be around another human being for two weeks. And she must emit a scent or something like it, because Cadmon always used to sneeze when she was in heat. It was really awkward; it isn't regular enough to predict, and he couldn't blow glass while he was sneezing. After the first time, I took her off into the countryside to get both of us away from people, but it was still a real disruption to our business."

"I can see how it would be," Lythande said. "At the moment, however, they are certainly giving you enough light to work by. But why are you working so late?"

Eirthe sighed, and rubbed her middle back. "The trade fair starts at mid-day tomorrow; the funeral used up half of what I planned to sell here, and there's still the coronation and wedding."

"Can I help?" Lythande asked. She wanted to talk to Eirthe, and they were unlikely to be disturbed here.

"Have you ever dipped candles before?"

"Actually, I have."

Eirthe's eyebrows rose skeptically. "Within the last century?"

"More like two," Lythande admitted. "But I think I can still manage to dip plain tapers."

Eirthe stood and gestured to the next rod. "Very well, give it a try."

Lythande picked up the rod by the ends, positioned it over the cauldron, and smoothly dipped the candles into the wax until they were covered to the same depth Eirthe had been using. Without pausing she pulled them straight up and held them over the pot. The new coat of wax ran down their sides and dripped off their bases. When the worst of the dripping stopped, she put the rod back on the rack, picked up the next one, and repeated the process.

"Not bad," Eirthe said. "If you can finish this batch, it will let me get a start on the ornamental candles for the marriage feast." She grinned and added, "We can talk while we work. Despite the gossip from the hall, I don't think you came looking for me for the sake of my beautiful brown eyes."

Lythande gave a mellow chuckle as she continued to dip candles. The repetitive motion was soothing, rather like playing finger exercises on her lute. "You are correct, Eirthe. I find I am woefully behind on the gossip here. Tell me about this marriage and what you know of the people involved."

Eirthe pulled a stool next to the fire, carried over a small work table, and set it up next to Lythande. One side of the table held several blocks of pure white wax with wicks coming out of their tops; the other side had a narrow tray holding a number of thin silver tools that were obviously used to carve the wax. She picked up the first block and, with a few swift strokes, carved it into the shape of a man, robed and crowned.

"Prince Tashgan you know: third son of Idriash, King and High Lord of Tschardain, trained in minstrelry, self-trained in wenching and drinking. His father was ill for decades, and the vizier ran the kingdom. He still does, although when Tashgan came home after his brothers' deaths he did take some slight interest in how his future kingdom was managed. Now that it *is* his, I expect he'll continue to let the vizier do most of the work. The trade fair is a good example of how things get done here: Tashgan decided he wanted his own trade fair, he told the vizier, and the vizier made sure that all of the details were taken care of so that what Tashgan wanted happened. Of course, the kingdom makes a handsome profit off it as well, which makes the vizier happy." She carved a good likeness of Tashgan's face into the wax she held, then placed it carefully in the exact center of the work table, setting her tools in a tray at the table's side.

Lythande, who had just finished dipping another rod of candles, froze in astonishment as Eirthe held her fingers on either side of the candle figure and chanted softly. A glow radiated and surrounded the candle, and when Eirthe fell silent and dropped her hands, it had become a perfect likeness of Tashgan, from the color of his skin, hair, and eyes to the gold of his crown.

"What are you doing?" she asked in astonishment,

even as the prickling running through the Blue Star on her forehead answered her. "I did not know you could work magic!"

Eirthe shrugged, picking up the candle. "It seems I always had some natural aptitude for it—Alnath has been with me since I was a small child. After all the confusion with the volcano when we were getting rid of the curse on me, I decided that I should learn more about it before I killed myself or someone else. So I spent a couple of years at the College in Northwander. Now I can do a few simple spells, and I have a much better idea of what to avoid doing if I want to stay out of trouble."

"Very sensible of you," Lythande said approvingly, remembering the incident to which Eirthe referred. The "confusion" with the volcano had occurred when the volcano demanded Lythande as a sacrifice to keep it from erupting. They had both had a narrow escape that time. "But making wax figures in the likeness of living people can be a dangerous thing."

"I know." Eirthe unlocked a metal trunk sitting in the far corner of her work area and took out a small wooden box lined with straw. She packed the Tashgan candle into it, closed it securely, and relocked the trunk. "I keep them locked up, with at least three salamanders guarding them at all times, and when they are burned at the feast, I'll be sitting near them. And these aren't magically similar representations of the people involved; they merely look like them. It's just a superficial likeness, not a true similarity. If it were not so, they could not be burned without harming the people they resemble."

"Are you sure?" Lythande asked. "Have you done this before?"

"Several times," Eirthe assured her. "I did one of Alnath and then several of myself before I tried doing one of anyone else. I don't give them away still formed;

they're always burned in my presence. Nobody has ever been harmed by these candles, and I intend to keep it that way." She spoke grimly, and Lythande remembered that it was Eirthe's refusal to make candles for a wizard who wanted to use them in an extortion scheme that had caused him to put his Cold Curse on her.

"I know you would never use them to harm someone," Lythande said soothingly. "But if they aren't used for magic, why do people want them made?"

"Vanity," Eirthe said simply. "It's a bit like having a portrait painted, but it also shows you're rich enough to pay for the work and then have it destroyed."

Lythande laughed. "I know that sort of vanity well. It enriches minstrels as well as craftsmen."

"That is the truth," Eirthe agreed, picking up a second plain white block and beginning to carve the folds of a long dress. "Now that Tashgan is to be king, he needs a queen. Or, rather, he needs heirs—legitimate ones—and he wants a useful alliance. So we have Princess

Velvet of Valantia. She's the twelfth of thirteen children, ten of them girls. Since Valantia and Tschardain have trade interests in common, her father gets rid of another daughter and can pay her dowry in trade concessions rather than hard cash."

"What does Tashgan get out of this?" Lythande asked. "Other than a beautiful princess, of course."

"Valantia's major product is their wines."

Lythande's lips twitched as she continued dipping candles in a steady rhythm. "I feel certain that was a major consideration."

"To Tashgan, at least," Eirthe agreed. "And the vizier approves, so the marriage should do well enough . . ." Her voice trailed off uncertainly. "Lythande?"

Lythande set down the last of the tapers she had been dipping and moved to Eirthe's side. While she had been working her way through the batch of tapers, Eirthe had finished another candle and set it in place.

"That is not Princess Velvet," Lythande said, studying the new figure.

Eirthe chewed on her lip, picked up the candle, and turned it over in her hands. "It's supposed to be," she said. "I've never had this happen before. Is there someone else's magic influencing me?"

Lythande took a deep breath, gripped the hilt of the magical dagger she wore under her robe, and cast her mind about the area. "There's quite a bit of magic in this castle," she said after a moment, "too much to identify it all without going into a full trance. But the simple answer is no. There is no magic influencing the work you are currently doing save your own."

"But that would mean that this is what Princess Velvet truly looks like—" Eirthe stared wide-eyed at Lythande. "Oh, Lord and Lady . . ."

"Finish the spell," Lythande ordered firmly. "Add the color."

Eirthe's hands trembled slightly as she put the figure

down, and she stared at it in silence for a long moment. In the quiet, Lythande heard the voices of the guards exchanging greetings on the walls of the outer court-yard and the soft whispers of salamanders basking in the faintly crackling fire. Then Eirthe placed her hands, now steady, about the figure and began to chant. When the glow died Lythande leaned forward, studying the figure intently.

"She's rather pretty," Eirthe ventured at last. "She has a kind face."

"And medium brown hair, pale gray eyes, and, I believe, freckles." Lythande sighed and straightened. "Can you imagine what Tashgan is going to say?"

"No," Eirthe said. "My imagination isn't that good."

"Why would anyone bespell Princess Velvet to change her appearance?" Lythande wondered. "Who would do such a thing? Who benefits by it?"

"Tashgan does," Eirthe said. "He likes beauty. And Velvet both benefits and is harmed by it."

"What do you mean?" Lythande asked.

"She probably wasn't given any choice about marrying him," Eirthe pointed out, "but her life will be vastly more pleasant if he likes her. He likes things which are beautiful, so he's disposed to like her now. But if she knows that her beauty is the result of a spell and not her true appearance, she knows that what he likes about her is an illusion, a lie." She shrugged. "I don't know Velvet well, but that would make *me* very unhappy."

Who here specializes in illusions? Lythande asked herself. *Where had she felt strange magic?* It came to her suddenly.

"Lady Mirwen," Lythande said aloud. "Make a candle of her, and tell me about her."

"It would have to be magically similar to tell us much of anything," Eirthe pointed out. "And I don't do magically similar candles."

"You know how, though," Lythande said. "You can

do it if you choose. I do not seek to harm the woman; I want only information. You may keep the candle and take what safeguards you wish."

"Very well," Eirthe said slowly. She opened the trunk again, packed the Velvet candle in a box, and buried it in the bottom layer. Then she picked up the next block of wax and began to carve it.

Lythande stood watching intently, ignoring the prickling sensation of the Blue Star on her forehead. Eirthe's brow furrowed in concentration, and she hummed something Lythande couldn't quite catch.

When the spell finished, the candle was a chimera, the face of Lady Mirwen on the body of a very fat spider. Lythande swallowed.

Eirthe regarded it in dismay. "Oh, dear," she sighed.

"I think we have our spell-caster," Lythande said. "Something about that woman bothered me from the moment I met her, and you have captured what I feel about her most clearly."

"So what do we do now?" Eirthe said faintly. Lythande studied her. Her face was pale and her hands were trembling.

"You lock these candles up, and we put the trunk in my room," Lythande said, dropping her voice to a whisper to make very certain that no one would overhear them. "Then we both go to bed. Tomorrow, we talk to Princess Velvet."

"What about the tapers?" Eirthe looked at the drying rack. "Oh, you've finished them. Can you pour the wax remaining in the cauldron into that mold over there?" She pointed to one of the row of wooden cubes she used to store and transport solid wax.

Lythande nodded, carried the cube next to the cauldron, and tipped the cauldron until the melted wax all ran into the mold. She was amused to notice that several of the baby salamanders came to help melt out the last drops. *Eirthe has quite a team working here.*

Eirthe locked the trunk, and each of them took a

handle. Escorted by a flight of salamanders, they took the back stairs to their rooms, where Lythande set the trunk against the stone wall at the far side of her room and spelled it to stay locked, closed, and bound to the wall. "It won't move unless the whole building comes down," she said reassuringly, "but if you want some of the salamanders to stay with it, I have no objection."

Eirthe, who had collapsed in the nearest chair as soon as she had set down her side of the trunk, nodded wearily. Alnath and two smaller balls of flame settled down on the trunk's lid.

Lythande, seeing that Eirthe had clearly reached the end of her resources for one day, marched the woman next door to her assigned room, stripped her swaying body down to her shift, and tucked her into bed. As she closed Eirthe's door behind her and returned to her own room, two guardsmen passed by at the end of the hallway. They eyed Lythande, saying nothing as they tried unsuccessfully to keep speculative grins from showing.

$\mathcal{E}$IRTHE RECOVERED QUICKLY; her knock on Lythande's door the next morning came at what Lythande considered an indecently early hour. Rolling out of bed and throwing on the concealing mage-robe, Lythande went to let the candlemaker in. Three salamanders flew from the trunk to mingle with the group accompanying Eirthe.

"They say that all was quiet last night," Eirthe said. "I am glad." Then she looked more closely at Lythande. "Did I wake you? The sun has been up for almost an hour."

"How nice for the sun," Lythande growled.

Eirthe's lips twitched. "Shall I order breakfast? You will probably feel better once you have eaten."

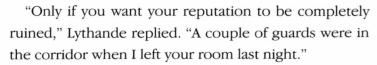

"Only if you want your reputation to be completely ruined," Lythande replied. "A couple of guards were in the corridor when I left your room last night."

Eirthe chuckled. "We can order breakfast from here and confuse them all. You need not worry about my reputation; Tashgan values me for my craft, not my virtue—or lack thereof." She crossed the room to tug on the bell-pull. "Besides," she added, "most of the people here already think I'm Tashgan's discarded mistress. Why else would I be housed in the castle at all, much less in such luxury?"

"I wondered about that myself," Lythande admitted. "Why *are* you housed in the castle?"

Eirthe laughed. "The first year the fair was held— before the vizier had the roads fixed—the weather was bad and my wagon got stuck in the mud a few miles away. There weren't very many people here then, so Tashgan allowed me to stay in the castle. The next year my room was ready for me when I arrived, and by the third year, of course, it had become a tradition for me to stay in the castle. I have no idea what, if anything, Tashgan was thinking, but I admit it's very nice to be indoors with servants to look after me."

"Perhaps you remind him of a time when he was young and carefree," Lythande said, "before he had to stay in one place and settle down."

"Probably," Eirthe agreed, going to the door to admit the servant she had summoned.

Lythande sank into a chair and pulled her hood to shadow her face while Eirthe dealt with the boy. She didn't move until Eirthe bolted the door behind the next servant who arrived five minutes later with their food.

Eirthe handed her a full plate. "The salamanders are all female," Eirthe said, "in case that matters to the rules you follow."

"It matters not," Lythande said, beginning to eat. Eirthe was right; food did make her feel at least a bit better. "It is only in the company of men that I am forbidden to eat or drink. If my companions are not human, their gender is not important."

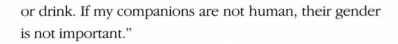

*A*FTER BREAKFAST THEY set off in search of Princess Velvet. "We need not worry about encountering Tashgan," Eirthe said. "He sleeps most of the morning."

"And Lady Mirwen?" Lythande asked skeptically.

"I sent Alnath to look. Mirwen is in the courtyard with the vizier, and the princess is in the solar."

"Not much of a chaperone, is she?" the magician commented.

"Just as well for us," Eirthe pointed out. "Alnath will keep watch and warn us if Lady Mirwen is coming."

"Very well," Lythande said. "Follow me and do not speak until we reach the solar." She led the way across the great hall and up the stairs to the solar, casting a minor glamour to keep anyone from seeing them.

Princess Velvet was indeed in the solar, curled up on a cushioned window ledge intent on the book she was reading. Lythande dropped the spell and cleared her throat. The princess squeaked in surprise and shoved the book under the cushion before looking up to see who had entered.

Eirthe laughed softly. "You need not hide the book on our account, Highness. I was here when you arrived; I know that half your baggage was books."

"Oh." Velvet looked at her with interest. "Do you like books?"

"Oh, yes," Eirthe said. "Half my things are books, too—they are much more interesting than clothes or jewels."

Velvet looked down at her dress, which was twisted around her legs and showing both her ankles. Blushing, she stood up and straightened her skirts. "I beg your pardon, Lord Magician," she said to Lythande.

"No need for that," Lythande said dryly. "I am not

young enough to be inflamed to madness by the sight of a woman's ankles." She realized belatedly that this was not reassuring; the princess looked as if she wished to sink through the floor.

Eirthe glared at Lythande. To the girl she said, "Lythande is several centuries old and no longer remembers how it feels to be young and easily embarrassed. Pay him no heed."

Velvet looked shocked at this lack of respect for a great magician. "Did you wish to speak to me, Lord Magician?" she asked Lythande.

"As it happens," Lythande replied, "I do. First, where is your lady-in-waiting?" She wanted to know if Mirwen planned to return soon.

Velvet's bland mask dropped and her face suddenly wore an astonishing look of cynicism. "Off chasing after the vizier. She will probably be gone for at least another hour—she has spent each morning since our arrival with him."

"Wants to be the power behind the throne, does she?" Lythande's centuries of experience suddenly came in quite handy.

Velvet shrugged. The blank-faced innocent look was completely gone now. "Why else would she leave home and come to a foreign land? I assure you that it was not for love of me."

"Has she cast any spells on you that you know of?" Lythande inquired.

Velvet's eyes rounded in surprise. "Not that I know of," she said uneasily. "You think I am bespelled." It was not a question.

"Eirthe." At Lythande's command Eirthe put the candle figure of Princess Velvet on the table in the center of the room. The sun, streaming in through the eastern window, cast a glow around it. Lythande turned to Velvet. "Can you tell us what this is, Princess?"

Velvet picked it up and turned it over in her hands. "Did you make this?"

Eirthe nodded.

The princess smiled. "It is an excellent likeness," she said. "You have a great gift."

"This looks like you?" Lythande asked.

Velvet looked at Lythande as if doubting the magician's sanity. "Yes, Lord Magician."

"Have you seen a mirror since you arrived here?" Lythande demanded.

"No." Velvet looked uneasy. "I never paid much attention to my looks. I have so many sisters that I never expected to marry, and in an arranged marriage, a princess's looks are much less important than her dowry. I do not even own a mirror—I'm the twelfth child, and mirrors are very expensive."

"True," Lythande agreed, "but they are useful in certain spells, so I always carry one." She pulled a small mirror from her belt pouch and handed it to the princess. "Look at yourself now."

Velvet stared into the mirror, gasped, and ran her

hand over her lips as if to be certain that it was her own reflection in the mirror. "I look like one of my father's mistresses," she exclaimed in horror. "They're the only women I know of who use face paint. Is this some sorcery of yours, Lord Magician?"

"Sorcery, yes," Lythande replied, "but not mine."

Velvet thrust the mirror back at Lythande, who took it and put it back into her belt pouch. "Can you remove this spell?" she asked anxiously. "I do not wish to go through the rest of my life looking like this! I look like a doll!"

"I could remove the spell quite easily," Lythande said, "but consider: this is how Lord Tashgan thinks you look." Velvet sank back onto the window ledge with a soft moan and buried her face in her hands. Lythande hoped the girl would not start crying. "And your lady-in-waiting doubtless had her reasons for changing your appearance," the mage added. That brought Velvet's

45

face out of her hands, her expression a thoughtful frown as she stared at Lythande and Eirthe.

"How did you find out that it was not my true appearance?" Velvet asked.

"Lord Tashgan asked me to make candles of both of you for the wedding feast," Eirthe explained. "And although I saw the illusion when I looked at you with my eyes, when I made the candle, it came out as you see." She gestured to the table, where Velvet had put the candle. "So I asked Lythande why what I made did not match what I had seen."

Velvet rose and walked around the table, studying the candle. "Could you make a candle of Lady Mirwen?" she asked. "I would like to know what *she* really looks like."

"I did," Eirthe said soberly. "It came out with her head on the body of a giant spider."

Velvet giggled. "You do indeed have a gift." Then she sobered. "But this isn't funny. She must be plotting something even more devious than her usual schemes."

She frowned. "We have not been here long, but even I can tell that the vizier is the one who truly runs the kingdom. And Lady Mirwen has always regarded people as expendable tools. My father does not like her; that is why she was able to gain his consent to accompany me to my new home. But he is a man—" She broke off, looking quickly at Lythande. "I mean to say that he does not see the side of her that she shows only in the women's quarters."

"You do not seem a stranger to palace intrigue yourself, Princess," Lythande said smoothly.

"But I am," Velvet said, twisting her hands nervously in front of her, "especially compared to Lady Mirwen. She has practiced it as long as I can remember, while I have done nothing but observe from the sidelines. I wasn't expected to marry, and I'm not a particular favorite of my father's, so I was not important enough to bother with."

"Interesting as all this is," Eirthe said, "I have candles to finish before the fair starts, and I need to get back to work. Are we certain that it was Lady Mirwen who changed your appearance?"

"I am certain," Velvet said grimly. "She made me wear a veil from the moment we approached the border until we arrived here, and while we were traveling she came to my room each night to brush my hair and help me prepare for bed—which she never bothered to do before." The princess frowned. "She still comes each night, but I doubt she will once I marry Tashgan." She looked up at Lythande. "Could she be using this illusion to distract him, to keep him from noticing her and wondering what she is doing?"

Eirthe picked up the candle and packed it back into its small straw-lined box. "If I wanted to distract Lord Tashgan, a beautiful girl is one of the surest methods."

Alnath returned, streaking through the open window

and landing on the wrist Eirthe held up for her. Lythande had no difficulty interpreting the salamander's message, too.

"Lady Mirwen is on her way here," she informed Velvet. "We must go."

"But—" Velvet began.

Lythande bowed. "Highness, if you think of anything more I should know, you may tell Eirthe. She has worked with me before and is to be trusted. And it would be better if your lady-in-waiting did not know that you and I have spoken together."

"Of course, Lord Magician." Velvet nodded regally, then added anxiously, "but you *will* remove this spell, will you not?"

Lythande smiled. "If you truly wish it, it will be my wedding gift to you."

"Start thinking of a way to explain it to Tashgan," Eirthe advised as Lythande pulled her toward the door. "Good luck!"

*E*IRTHE SPENT THE rest of the morning making candles and moving her stock around until she was satisfied that it was displayed to its best advantage. Meanwhile, Lythande prowled the castle, the outbuildings, and the fairgrounds, stopping occasionally to play her lute and sing a few songs where people gathered, always listening to whatever was being said around her. Unfortunately, while she found some of it mildly interesting, none of it was any particular help.

The fair opened formally at noon, with a speech of welcome from the vizier. After the formalities ended, Lythande followed him as he went through the fair, speaking to each merchant and checking for any last-minute problems. She was pleased to observe that he appeared to be well liked and competent.

Not that Tashgan isn't well liked, Lythande thought to herself, *but his areas of competence are rather lim-*

ited. He needs a good vizier, and he's very lucky to have this one.

LYTHANDE SPENT THE next three days wandering the fairground, looking at all the different merchandise, thinking of possible illusions for the Marriage Games, and pausing frequently to play for fairgoers. She stopped to see Eirthe at least once each day and was pleased to find the candlemaker selling her stock faster than she could make it. It seemed to Lythande that Eirthe's candles would light every home in the kingdom at least through the winter, if not until next Yule.

On the fourth day, Prince Tashgan's old lute arrived. Lythande, who was standing a short distance from Eirthe's booth, was surprised to see a woman, past her first youth but still very beautiful, approach the candlemaker's stall. She wore the hood of her cloak thrown back, revealing braided loops of long golden hair, and her cloak hung open in the front, showing off a dress of green silk with gold dragons embroidered on it. The woman certainly did not appear to feel the cold. Lythande, recognizing her at once even after ten years and many adventures, *knew* she didn't feel the cold. Then again, she wasn't really a woman.

"Mistress Candlemaker," the woman greeted Eirthe. "I see you have been blessed." A wave of her hand indicated the salamanders.

"Lady Beauty," Eirthe said with a smile. "How good to see you again. Yes, Alnath had babies last summer. Aren't they wonderful?"

"They're lovely," Beauty said with unmistakable sincerity. "Speaking of children, I hear that Lord Tashgan is finally going to marry. Have you seen his bride? What is she like?"

"Very young," Eirthe replied, "but she seems like a

nice girl." She shrugged. "It's a political arrangement, of course."

"Of course." The lady in green smiled, showing rather a lot of teeth. "I must go to the castle and congratulate the dear boy." She turned away and walked off, giving Lythande an excellent view of Tashgan's lute case slung across her back.

Lythande gave Beauty plenty of time to get beyond earshot before approaching Eirthe. "What do you know of that creature?" she inquired, careful to keep her voice low.

"Lady Beauty?" Eirthe asked, looking at Lythande in surprise. "She's an old friend of Tashgan's; she comes here every year at this time. She's an excellent musician—perhaps you saw the lute?"

"Eirthe," Lythande said urgently. "How long does she stay here when she comes?"

"Five days," Eirthe said. "Why? Do you need to avoid her?"

"Where else have you seen her?"

"She comes to the fair at Old Gandrin each year," Eirthe replied promptly, "and she was in Northwander at mid-summer both the years I was there." She frowned. "Lythande, what's wrong? You called her a creature—is she not human?"

"Does she seem so to you?"

"Not a normal human, certainly," Eirthe said softly. "I've known her for years now and she hasn't aged. And her clothes never get dirty. Most people don't travel dressed as she does—and she's quite fond of Alnath, which is unusual. I thought she must be some kind of mage—she *does* have magic, I know that." She lowered her voice even more. "If she's not human, what is she?"

"A were-dragon," Lythande said grimly.

"Oh, dear." Eirthe looked wide-eyed along the path Beauty had taken. "That would explain why she and

Alnath get along so well." She frowned in concern. "Is she an enemy of yours, Lythande?"

"I don't know," Lythande admitted. "I gave her the lute, but I thought she'd be able to remove the binding spell easily . . . certainly after all these years . . ."

"What binding spell?" Eirthe demanded.

"When Tashgan's brothers were still alive and he was not the heir," Lythande explained, "they had Ellifanwy, the Court Magician here, put a binding spell on his lute. It governed both his route and the amount of time he spent in each place. He came here for five days at Yule-tide each year, passed through the fair at Old Gandrin each spring, spent mid-summer in Northwander, and then made his way back here, only to start the same route anew."

Eirthe's eyes went even wider. "And Beauty is following that route, as she has done every year since—" She chewed on her lower lip, obviously trying to reckon the years.

"—since the year Prince Tashgan came to me at Old Gandrin and asked me to take the binding spell off his lute," Lythande finished the sentence. "Ellifanwy was dead by then—she died in a were-dragon's lair, oddly enough—and he was in a hurry because his brothers had just died. I traded lutes with him, intending to remove the spell at my leisure. Of course, I was following his route in the meantime—"

"I'll bet *that* was interesting," Eirthe said with a grin.

"Very," Lythande said dryly. "In any event, I still had not removed the spell when the lute led me to a house in the middle of a swamp. Beauty lived there. Apparently she was quite fond of Tashgan—"

"She still is," Eirthe interjected.

"—and she was not at all pleased to see me in his place," Lythande continued, "although she did calm down somewhat once I convinced her I had not killed him."

Eirthe snickered.

Lythande glared at her. "Tashgan mentioned her when he gave me the lute—not that he told me anything useful about her, of course; he just said, 'Give my love to Beauty.' So I made up a grand tale about his sacrificing his love for her to his duty as his father's heir, and I gave her the lute to remember him by. I really didn't think it would bind her—certainly not for almost ten years!"

"She's been coming here every year," Eirthe said, "but that doesn't *prove* she's bound. She could be doing it of her own free will."

"I hope you're right," Lythande said. "I had best go up to the castle and find out. If she's angry with me, things could get very awkward."

"Wait until the fair ends," Eirthe said. "It's only another hour, and I want to go with you. I wouldn't miss this for the world!"

$\mathcal{B}$Y THE TIME the fair ended and Eirthe had inventoried and packed up her remaining stock, it was rather more than an hour. Lythande, however, was in no particular hurry to confront Beauty, so she waited until Eirthe and the salamanders were ready to accompany her.

They entered the back of the great hall quietly. Tashgan and Velvet still sat side by side at the high table, with Lady Mirwen on Velvet's right. The green cloak draped over the back of the empty chair at Tashgan's left hand indicated where Beauty had dined, but now she sat on a stool at the front of the dais, playing an intricate melody on her lute.

Lythande was immediately impressed by two things: the fingering required by Beauty's song was difficult enough to challenge any musician, and every single person in the hall was listening with rapt attention. No one was fidgeting, or looking bored, or whispering to a neighbor, and no one had so much as turned a head when Lythande and Eirthe entered. Lythande clasped the two daggers concealed beneath her cloak and checked for the presence of magic—long years of being a traveling minstrel had taught her that this sort of music was most definitely *not* the way to enthrall an audience—but the only active spell was the one Lady Mirwen was using to change Velvet's appearance. Even a more thorough check for the presence of potential magic picked up only what Lythande already knew: the salamanders, Eirthe's talent, Lady Mirwen, and the magic that Beauty had by virtue of being a were-dragon.

The song died away into silence and everyone applauded, even the armsmen and the servants. Lythande, joining in the applause, whispered to Eirthe, "Is her playing always so well appreciated?"

"Invariably," Eirthe murmured back, still clapping along with the rest of the hall's occupants. "Lady Beauty *likes* to be appreciated, and she is known to have quite a temper."

"Ah, there you are, Lythande!" Lord Tashgan had just looked up and spotted them. "What do you think of Lady Beauty's playing?"

"Most impressive." Lythande strode boldly forward and bowed to Tashgan and Velvet, then bent over the hand that Beauty extended. "My compliments, Lady Beauty. I applaud both your skill and your courage; I would not dare to undertake such a sophisticated piece in general company."

Beauty smiled blandly at Lythande. "Thank you, Lord Magician." Her fingers squeezed Lythande's briefly before she released them. "I come here each year to celebrate the Yule feast, and I flatter myself that the audience only improves in its ability to appreciate good music."

"That requires no flattery, Lady," Lythande said, inclining her head respectfully. "The response of your audience is proof of the correctness of your opinion."

"Perhaps you would consent to play a duet with me," Beauty said, smiling sweetly. Lythande could almost hear her thinking: *I know your secret, and you know I know, and you wonder what I shall do with the knowledge. How amusing.*

"It would be my honor," Lythande said, bowing again.

"Excellent!" Tashgan said. "You there," he pointed at the nearest page. "A stool for Lythande."

The boy ran to do as he was told, and a few minutes later Lythande was sitting knee-to-knee with Beauty, tuning her lute to match the were-dragon's.

"Now what shall we play?" Beauty mused aloud. She played a few bars of music, her fingers flying over the strings. "Do you know this one? I believe that your voice is high enough to manage it."

Lythande, joining obediently in the introduction, did indeed recognize the piece, and she very much hoped that no one else did. It was an old song of a love between two women that endured even when both of

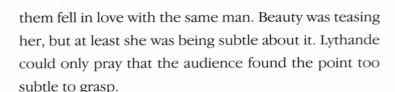

them fell in love with the same man. Beauty was teasing her, but at least she was being subtle about it. Lythande could only pray that the audience found the point too subtle to grasp.

Enthusiastic applause followed the song, and Beauty started right into a piece often used as a showpiece by competing musicians. The first player would lay down a complicated melody and the second would improvise and elaborate upon it, then the first would play an even more complicated version of what the second had just done, and so forth. Lythande was prepared to let Beauty win the duel if she could so do without being obvious and was slightly chagrined to discover that it was not necessary. Beauty was good enough to outplay Lythande, though it did take her the better part of an hour to do so.

"We must do this again, dear boy," Beauty said to Lythande as they rose to their feet and bowed together to Lord Tashgan and graciously accepted his praise. "It is not often that I have the pleasure of playing with someone who comes so close to keeping up with me."

Lythande, still buoyed up in the exaltation of playing really good music, grinned happily. "It would be my pleasure, Lady Beauty." She gave the were-dragon a courtly bow.

"Indeed." Beauty looked around the hall and chuckled softly. "I think perhaps we were all caught up in the music's spell," she said. "Look, the candles have burned low and—" She lowered her voice to reach only to Lythande's ears. "Tashgan's little bride looks ready to fall asleep where she sits."

"It can't possibly have been the music," Lythande whispered back.

"I suspect it's more the strangeness of being in a new land for the first time," Beauty said softly, "and, of course, the spell on her saps her energies somewhat."

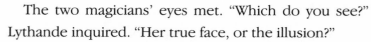

The two magicians' eyes met. "Which do you see?" Lythande inquired. "Her true face, or the illusion?"

Beauty's laugh rivaled the wind-chimes that were sold at the fair. "Why, both, of course." She turned away to pack up her lute, and Lythande followed her example.

By the time Lythande reached her room, the energy from the music was wearing off, and she felt ready to fall asleep in the doorway. But first she checked to make certain that no one had tried to disturb the box with Eirthe's spelled candles. To her relief, things were just as she had left them that morning.

Eirthe tapped on her door and came in with a tray of bread, cheese, and dried fruit. "Try to eat something before you fall asleep," she said. "You look even more tired than I feel—and I'd like to sleep for a week! At least we have one day to rest before the wedding."

"It's a good thing we do," Lythande said. "I'm going to need it."

THE DAY OF the wedding was beautiful and unseasonably warm. By the time Lythande woke, the sun was halfway up the cloudless bright blue sky, and the air had only enough chill in it to be refreshing. The wind was the gentlest of breezes. Lythande sat on the windowsill, basking in the sun, ignoring the salamander who left the group guarding the trunk with the wedding candles and streaked past her into the open air.

A short time later there was a tap on her door. Lythande opened it to find Eirthe had brought breakfast.

"Thank you, Eirthe," she said. "Please join me—or have you eaten already?"

"Hours ago," Eirthe replied with a smile, "but I wouldn't mind a bit more fruit. I've just finished setting out all the tapers in the great hall. It's going to be the best-lit room you have ever seen."

"Are the wedding preparations completed, then?" Lythande had spent the previous day in her room, resting and practicing illusions. Eirthe had brought her food at regular intervals, but had left her alone otherwise, so Lythande didn't know the current state of the castle. She knew Eirthe would have informed her of anything obviously crucial, so she assumed that things had been quiet—at least magically.

"Very nearly," Eirthe replied, smothering a yawn. "You did well to stay out of the mess yesterday— between the tear-down of the fair and the preparations for the wedding, it was the most chaotic mess I've ever seen. Most of the fair folk are pretty efficient, but the castle staff doesn't put on a wedding every year. And from all the fuss and bother, I think some of them deliberately left things until the last moment so they could run around and yell at other people and seem busy and important."

"Does that include the vizier?" Lythande asked curiously.

"Fortunately he had delegated the wedding preparations to the head steward," Eirthe said, "because Lady Mirwen kept running to him all day with crisis after crisis, and he didn't have time to do anything yesterday except deal with her."

"Interesting," Lythande mused. "I should think that sort of behavior would be likely to give him a dislike for her."

"Perhaps not," Eirthe said. "She certainly didn't miss a single opportunity to tell him how wonderful he was and how she didn't know how she could have managed to cope without him."

"What did you do, follow her around all day?"

"Of course not." Eirthe smiled innocently. "I was dipping candles in the courtyard almost the entire day. Ask anyone." She grinned. "I had the salamanders keep watch. We've been here long enough now that no one pays much heed to them as long as they don't get too close—and have you ever noticed how seldom people look *up*? And no one looks closely at the wall sconces; one of the babies has spent several days in Velvet's room impersonating a candle flame. He's still there, in fact; I think he likes her." She looked thoughtful. "I wonder how Tashgan would react if I gave his bride a salamander for a wedding gift?"

Lythande chuckled. "I suspect that would depend on where it wanted to sleep at night."

Eirthe popped the last piece of fruit into her mouth, swallowed it, and licked her fingers. "I'll think about it." She rose to her feet. "I had better go and dress for the ceremony. Have you decided what illusions you'll use for the Games?"

"I have a number of possibilities," Lythande said, "but I expect to do a lot of improvisation once the duel gets started."

"I expect it will be very interesting," Eirthe said. "I'll see you at the ceremony."

THE WEDDING WAS held at the entrance to the castle, so as many people as wanted to could witness their ruler's marriage. Tashgan was resplendent in a long cloth-of-gold tunic, while Velvet wore a dress of deep sapphire velvet with a matching headdress that completely covered her hair. A pale blue silk veil attached to the crown of the headdress covered her face. The wedding party—the priest, the bride and groom, and their chief witnesses—stood on the steps, and spectators crowded the courtyard. The vizier was the witness for Tashgan, as Lythande had expected, but she was surprised to see Lady Beauty standing with Velvet. She looked around the courtyard, but did not see Lady Mirwen anywhere.

"Do you know where Mirwen is?" she whispered to Eirthe, who was standing next to her.

"Still in the great hall, I guess," Eirthe replied. "That's where she was when I came out, but I thought she'd be out for the ceremony."

"It would appear that she has better things to do than to watch her charge get married," Lythande said dryly.

"Several of the salamanders are in there," Eirthe said reassuringly. "I'll find out what she was doing as soon as the ceremony is over."

$\mathcal{B}$UT AS SOON as the ceremony ended the marriage-feast started, and Lythande's status meant that she was stuck at the high table with Tashgan and the vizier. Fortunately it appeared to be the custom to separate, by the full length of the table, the champions of the Marriage Games, so the vizier sat to Lady Mirwen's left, with Velvet on his left, followed by Tashgan, Beauty, and Lythande.

This left Lythande with Lady Beauty as a dinner companion, but at least she was spared having to make conversation to both sides. She applied herself to toying with her food, though of course she could not actually eat, while Beauty complimented Tashgan on his bride's beauty—as if he had anything to do with that—and joked about how eager he must be to begin his duties as a husband. Tashgan laughed, agreed with everything she said, and drank his wine. Beauty reminded him to eat: "You'll need your strength, dear boy, and 'tis well known that too much wine dulls the performance . . ."

As Tashgan obediently began to eat, Beauty turned her attention to Lythande. "I hear that you, dear boy, are to be Tashgan's champion in a contest of magic after dinner."

Was there a twinge of jealousy in her voice? Lythande wasn't sure. At least she seemed willing to keep Lythande's secret.

"That is true," Lythande admitted, then succumbed to curiosity. "Tell me, Lady Beauty; do you call everyone 'dear boy'?"

"Frequently," Beauty said with a smile. "It's so much

easier than remembering names; people come and go so quickly, don't you think? It also reduces the chance of my miscalling someone—by the wrong name, I mean," she said, looking deliberately bland.

"Quite." Lythande kept her voice and face equally bland.

"I do believe that your little friend is looking for you," Beauty added, indicating a salamander hovering in the doorway.

"So it would seem," Lythande murmured. "If you would excuse me for a moment, my lady?"

Beauty smiled and bent closer, obviously willing to enter into the conspiracy. "If anyone asks, you've gone to the privy."

Lythande nodded and slipped from the room as quietly as possible.

In fact the salamander did lead her in the direction of the privies, where she met Eirthe, apparently returning from there to the hall.

"She was casting some sort of spell on the contest area," Eirthe said quickly, smiling as if they were exchanging greetings. "Something fairly elaborate, but the salamanders couldn't give me any details aside from the fact that she used her own candles and not any of mine! *That* they noticed."

"Well, I'm sure we'll find out the details soon," Lythande said with resignation. *I was afraid this day was going to be interesting.*

"No doubt," Eirthe agreed, continuing back to the hall. Lythande went to the privies before going back herself; the easiest way to carry off deception was to make as much of it as possible the truth.

$\mathcal{T}$HE FEAST CONTINUED for several hours. Lythande refused all offers of additional food and wine; not only could she not eat here, she knew she needed to be alert for the work to come.

Finally Tashgan stood up to announce the contest.

"It is the custom of my bride's people," he began, "to have a contest of magical illusions to celebrate a wedding. The two champions will vie with each other to create the most fantastic and beautiful illusion, and you, my friends, will be the judges." Waiting for the applause to die down, he continued, "The champions will be Lady Mirwen for Valantia and Lythande for Tschardain. Let the Games begin!"

As Lythande rose, Lady Mirwen strode quickly to the area cleared for the contest and faced Tashgan. "Lord Tashgan, as I told you when you first proposed this sacrilege, these Games are for women. No man may be a champion in the Marriage Games. I have, therefore, bespelled this area so that only a woman can work magic in it." Lythande froze in place, but kept her face impassive as Mirwen gloated. "Unless your 'champion' can prove himself a woman, you will have to concede the Games—or find a *suitable* champion."

"Lythande?" Tashgan turned to her. "Can you remove her spell?"

Lythande hoped her laugh did not sound as forced as it felt. "Easily, Lord Tashgan. But I'm sorry to have to inform you that the quickest way to do so is to undo *all* her spells, which will, of course, make her unable to compete in the Games." *And will, of course, remove the illusion from Velvet as well. I'm not certain that Lady Mirwen wants that to happen just yet.*

It seemed that Lythande was correct on that last point, for Lady Mirwen looked distinctly nervous. She had just opened her mouth, presumably to offer to cancel the spell herself, when. Beauty intervened.

"Lord Tashgan," she said, rising to her feet. "I ask a boon. Let *me* be your champion!"

Tashgan looked at Lythande, who could appreciate his dilemma. He certainly must know enough about

75

Beauty that he would never wish to offend her, but he wasn't certain just how powerful—and likely to take offense—Lythande might be. But Lythande had excellent reasons for wishing to keep Beauty happy as well.

"If Lady Beauty wishes it," Lythande said promptly, "I would be well content to relinquish my place to her. I have the greatest respect for her magical abilities."

"And Lady Mirwen would have no cause to complain of any sacrilege," Beauty pointed out.

"Very well," Tashgan said. "Lady Beauty shall be my champion. Lythande shall act as referee." Lythande gallantly pulled Beauty's chair back and escorted her from the dais before returning to her own place at the head table.

Lady Mirwen faced Beauty with the self-satisfied look of a spoiled child who had gotten her own way once again. "This is much better, don't you think? Men shouldn't try to play at magic; it finds its highest and truest expression in the human female. No one can deny that."

"I wouldn't stake *my* life on that," Beauty said, smiling enigmatically.

Mirwen obviously didn't understand that statement, so she ignored it. She waved her hands in an elaborate showy pattern and chanted something that was clearly intended to be a spell. Lythande, from her long life and extensive musical background, recognized it as a very old students' drinking song, old enough that the language was no longer spoken in that form. From the twitching of Beauty's lips, Lythande was sure that she too had identified the "spell." But Beauty stood quietly, allowing her opponent to create the first illusion.

A meadow with bright green grass dotted with brilliantly colored flowers suddenly hid the floor, and a crystal blue pond filled the foreground. It was quite pretty, Lythande had to admit. A line of trees made a backdrop for the scene and concealed Mirwen, which Lythande thought improved the aesthetic appeal considerably.

Beside the pond sat two figures: Velvet—a copy of the illusion, which was still on the real princess—and a younger-looking and rather heroically idealized Tashgan.

And that's probably exactly what he thinks he does look like, Lythande thought. *Clever move. Not brilliant, but clever. Not bad for an opening illusion, and quite suitable for a wedding.*

The murmurs of appreciation in the hall died away as everyone waited to see what Beauty would do to answer this. When the hall was completely silent, Beauty began.

A glittering silvery mist rose up from the pond, hiding the figures and the landscape. Lights flickered within the mist for several minutes, and then a breeze came out of nowhere and blew the mist away. Gasps of astonishment and pleasure swept through the hall. Beauty had made the illusion larger, so that everyone could see it, and she had added a castle of glistening white marble, carved into fantastic shapes and ornamentation. As the spectators oohed and aahed, the illusory "sky" changed from blue into a beautiful multicolored sunset, followed by darkness, broken by lights shining from the castle and reflecting off the water of the pond. The entire banquet hall darkened as well, enabling the audience to see the illusion better and without distraction. Then dawn came, with more colors, soft pastels deepening as "day" dawned. As the light brightened around the figures of Tashgan and Velvet, Lythande gave an appreciative chuckle. The figure of Velvet was pregnant.

"Fast work," a man's voice called from somewhere in the hall. That got a round of laughter from nearly everyone, including Tashgan.

Lythande thought that she heard Lady Mirwen hissing through her teeth, but she couldn't be sure because the castle blocked her view of the woman.

Beauty stepped back and allowed Mirwen to take her next turn. A sudden darkness hid the scene, and when it lifted just as suddenly—and nowhere near as artistically as Beauty's idealized sunset and sunrise—Velvet and Tashgan had two children: a sturdy boy toddling around at the edge of the pond and a baby in Velvet's arms. Both children had the same perfect beauty as the illusion Velvet wore.

Not the best move, Lythande thought, listening to mutters from the hall. *Children who favor their mother so completely could be fathered by anyone. It would be more politic to have at least one of them resemble Tashgan.*

Beauty seemed to share Lythande's opinion. She gave an audible sniff of disdain as she moved forward to take her next turn. The boy grew from a toddler into a young boy and, as he grew, his form changed so that he looked very much like Tashgan. The baby wriggled out of its mother's lap, crawled to the edge of the pond and surveyed its reflection in the water, tilting its little head to one side as if in thought. Then it reached forward with a chubby little hand and splashed water on its face. The coloring and features changed as if a layer of paint had been washed away. The little girl who sat up and began to gather flowers for a chain had brown hair, grey eyes, and freckles. She was cute, and she looked very much the way Velvet must have looked at that age.

Lythande looked around. At the high table Velvet was laughing, and Tashgan was smiling.

Mirwen became visible through the towers of the castle as she moved from behind it to stand just behind the trees on her side of the illusion. She looked furious. Obviously she had not expected anyone to see through the illusion she had placed on Velvet, much less to let her know that they had done so.

"How dare you!" she snarled softly.

But Beauty wasn't done yet. From the edge of the patch of illusion, animals began to appear. At first they were fairly ordinary: a sapphire blue bird flew to perch on the illusory Velvet's shoulder, picking up the color of her eyes; an elegant sleek golden hound came to sit at Tashgan's side. The complexity of the illusion increased: a group of deer in all the colors of the rainbow came to drink from the pool, then blue-and-green ducks and silver swans floated across its surface, and lastly a pure white unicorn with a silver horn spiraling outward from the center of its forehead walked up to the little girl, dipping its head so that she could put her flower chain around its neck.

Mirwen raised her arms dramatically and snapped out a few words in a language Lythande didn't recognize. It still sounded like a curse. *Oh-oh,* Lythande thought, *this is getting ugly.*

A pack of black wolves came out of the pond and rushed to surround the unicorn and the girl, fangs bared. The girl backed up against the unicorn's side, and the unicorn defended itself as best it could with kicks at any wolf who got too close, but they were badly outnumbered. A couple of wolves darted in to attack, and the unicorn was bleeding by the time it beat them back.

This is too much. Lythande rose to her feet and shouted, "Hold!"

All action in the scene froze as Mirwen turned to Lythande. "What is your problem?" she snarled.

"The game being played here, Lady Mirwen, is *not* 'My illusion can kill your illusion,'" Lythande said sternly. "This is not a magical duel. You appear to be forgetting that."

"It is not your place to interfere," Lady Mirwen snapped. "I was weaving illusions before you were born!"

"I doubt that very much," Lythande said calmly. "Lord Tashgan named me referee for these Games. You are supposed to be making something beautiful, not causing

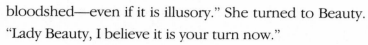

bloodshed—even if it is illusory." She turned to Beauty. "Lady Beauty, I believe it is your turn now."

"Of course, dear boy," Beauty said, smiling. She stepped forward and began to work. First she dissolved a section of illusion, revealing Lady Mirwen to the audience, and grew the image of a tree over the rival sorceress. It wasn't a beautiful tree; it was gnarled and twisted and actually quite ugly—and very clearly what Mirwen *would* look like if she were a tree. Laughter echoed around the hall as people caught the joke. The Mirwen tree twisted, trying to glare at everyone who was laughing, but Beauty waved a slender hand and water fell from above, covering the tree completely. Beauty looked at it and inhaled sharply, and the water froze, coating the tree with ice, which caught the light from Eirthe's candles and glittered in a flickering pattern.

That's as close to beautiful as Mirwen is ever likely to get, Lythande thought.

Beauty turned her attention to the wolves surrounding the unicorn and smiled again. She waved her hand, and the wolves were transformed into cuddly black puppies. They frolicked around, emitting enthusiastic little yelps, and butting at the girl's ankles before darting off to play with the boy.

Now healed, the unicorn, with the girl still at its side, walked forward to dip its horn in the pool. The pool spread toward Lady Beauty until it touched the hem of her skirt, and she began to transform as well. Her arms dropped to touch her sides briefly before sweeping upward and back, and as they moved, her green and gold sleeves changed to wings with scales so bright they seemed made of gold and emeralds. Her body grew, her face elongated, and before anyone could so much as blink, a dragon stood in her place, towering over the pool and dominating the scene.

The soft gasps and hushed attention of the spectators were more of an accolade than any applause. The audience waited in fascination to see what would happen next. Even Lythande sat transfixed, and Tashgan was scarcely breathing.

The dragon puffed out its cheeks and blew out a soft pale flame which melted the ice covering the tree. Lady Mirwen snapped out of the illusion and stalked through the line of trees to confront her adversary.

"The champions are *not* supposed to be part of the illusions!" she snapped. "And I don't know what you think you've turned yourself into, but I assure you that it's *ugly*! Didn't anyone tell you that these illusions are supposed to be beautiful?"

"I am a dragon," Beauty replied calmly, "and I *am* beautiful. If beauty is the main criterion of this contest, however, I can readily see why you disqualify yourself—although as an ice-covered tree you had a certain charm."

"You are hideous, scaly, and altogether loathsome!"

Mirwen snarled. "You call yourself a sorceress? A simple hedge-witch has better taste!"

"I really couldn't say," Beauty mused aloud. "It's been so long since I've eaten a hedge-witch that I'm afraid I've forgotten the precise taste of one. Anyway, once they are properly broiled, most humans taste pretty much alike."

"You're not funny!" Mirwen was almost screaming now. "I won't let you make a fool out of me!"

"My dear girl," Beauty replied, obviously quite amused, "I don't have to. You do it so well yourself."

Even Lythande chuckled at that, though she doubted that she could be heard above the roar of laughter coming from the rest of the hall. Tashgan had almost doubled over, and now Lythande could see Velvet beyond him. The girl was well trained, one had to admit that; she was still sitting upright with a reasonably composed face. Having a side view, Lythande could see clearly where Velvet was biting the inside of her cheek

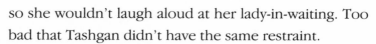

so she wouldn't laugh aloud at her lady-in-waiting. Too bad that Tashgan didn't have the same restraint.

Unfortunately, being laughed at was something Mirwen obviously could not tolerate. She drew a dagger from her sleeve and rushed at Beauty. Lythande moved to intercept her, just in time to catch the edge of the blast of flame that incinerated Lady Mirwen. The flames, however, were carefully angled to avoid the high table, so they missed Lythande's face and struck the side of her cloak. Since it was fireproof, there was no damage, except to Lady Mirwen—and to Velvet.

In the instant Mirwen turned to a pile of ash, the illusion spell on Velvet vanished. Lythande and Velvet were face to face, and as soon as Velvet saw Lythande's expression, she realized what had happened. Demonstrating the quick intelligence Lythande had always suspected she possessed, the girl gasped and did an excellent simulation of a faint, landing in a graceful sprawl on the floor with one of her long trailing sleeves completely hiding her face. Eirthe's salamanders promptly clustered around the princess, their dazzling colors making it even harder to see her clearly.

Beauty returned to human form without even a hair out of place. Ignoring the total confusion in her audience, she banished the illusion with a negligent wave of her hand and rushed to join Lythande on the dais. Eirthe came around from the other end of the dais to join her salamanders in hovering over Velvet's supine body.

"What happened?" Tashgan asked, looking down at Velvet with concern. "Is she all right?"

"She just saw her governess die, my Lord," the vizier said, looking down at Velvet. "It is bound to have been a shock." He frowned at the confusion. "Can someone get those salamanders out of the way?"

"They like the princess," Eirthe explained. "They are simply trying to protect her."

"And quite successfully, too," Lythande remarked.

"While they're there, nobody is going to step on the poor girl. By your leave, Lord"—she bowed to Tashgan—"Eirthe and I will take your wife to her room. She's just seen her only companion from home incinerated right before her; she will need time to compose herself."

"Yes, of course," Tashgan said. He looked confused.

"It's a bit much for him to take in all at once," Beauty said, pouring a goblet of wine. "Drink this, dear boy, and just sit quietly while they tend to your wife." She shot a sharp look at Lythande, who obediently moved to pick up Velvet, thankful that the girl was slender and easy to carry. As she followed Eirthe towards Velvet's room, she could hear Beauty demanding that someone fetch her lute. *Good,* Lythande thought. *By the time she's done playing, this crowd won't know—or care—what they just saw.*

When they reached Velvet's room, Lythande dropped the girl unceremoniously on her bed. The salamanders moved off to one side.

"All right, Princess, you can wake up now."

Velvet's eyes snapped open instantly, but when she tried to sit up she began to sway. Lythande had to steady her.

"Not so fast," Eirthe said, handing Velvet a goblet of watered wine. "It has been a rather eventful day for you."

"I'm all right," Velvet insisted. "I didn't really faint."

"You didn't?" Eirthe asked, startled.

Lythande chuckled. "If she ever tires of being Lady of Tschardain, she can go on the stage. That was as neatly acted as anything I've ever seen. Excellent timing, too."

"But why—" Eirthe started to say, and then realized. "Of course! The spell was broken when Mirwen died."

"It was, wasn't it?" Velvet asked. "I thought it must be when I saw the way Lythande was looking at me—am I back to normal?"

"Oh, yes," Eirthe assured her. "You look just like the first candle I made of you."

"The first candle?" Lythande asked.

"I made a second one to match the illusion," Eirthe explained. "I wasn't sure what she'd look like by the time it came to display them."

"What about the candle of Mirwen?" Lythande asked.

"I still have that one," Eirthe replied. "I'll burn it down tonight. I didn't want to do it while she was alive because that one *is* magically similar."

"Could I have it?" Velvet asked. "I'd like to burn it myself."

Eirthe looked at Lythande, who nodded. "Of course, Princess, if it will make you feel better."

"I'm sure it will," Velvet said grimly. "Now, about my appearance—"

She broke off as Tashgan walked in, followed by Beauty and the vizier.

"Princess," the vizier began formally, "I hope that you are recovered."

Velvet opened her mouth to reply, but before she could say a single word, Tashgan gasped.

"What happened to you?" he asked in horror.

"What?" The vizier looked at Tashgan in bewilderment.

"Look at her face!" Tashgan burst out.

The vizier, obviously puzzled, looked at Velvet, squinting in an effort to see her more clearly. "What's wrong with it?" he said. "It looks fine to me."

He's short-sighted, Lythande realized. *To him she still looks the same. Too bad Tashgan isn't.* "Lady Mirwen cast a spell on her," Lythande explained quickly.

"You can reverse it, can't you?" Tashgan asked urgently. "You said you could undo all that woman's magic."

"Yes," Lythande said carefully, "I can change her back to the way she was this morning, if she wishes it. But the spell only alters her outward appearance. She's not ill or injured, and she's still exactly the same person she was before. Do her looks matter that much?"

"Yes, of course they do!" Tashgan snapped. Velvet looked down at her lap. "I can't have people saying that marrying me turned her into a hag."

Eirthe drew her breath in an outraged gasp and moved to stand nose to nose with Tashgan. "She is *not* a hag, and that is a stupid and cruel thing to say!"

"I see nothing wrong with your wife's appearance," Beauty said calmly.

"Lythande." Tashgan was obviously trying for a man-to-man rapport. "You understand. You know how important beautiful surroundings are to me."

Lythande sighed and looked at Velvet. The girl looked up, blinking back tears, and nodded. "Yes, Tashgan," Lythande said with another sigh, "I do understand. I can change her face back. But keeping her beautiful depends on you."

"What do you mean?" Tashgan asked.

"The thing most important to the beauty of a married woman is her husband's love," Lythande explained.

"You have to treat her with love and respect—and you have to keep doing so, or her beauty will not last."

"Lord Tashgan, surely there are more important things to worry about. Does it really matter what she looks like?" the vizier asked impatiently.

"Yes, it does," Tashgan said promptly. He looked appealingly at Lythande. "Change her back, please, and I shall do whatever I have to in order for the spell to hold."

"If your wife is willing," Lythande said.

"As my husband desires," Velvet replied promptly. "It might be best, however, if all of you returned to the feast. I feel sure that there has been enough disruption for one day."

"Quite right, your highness." The vizier nodded and left the room.

"She's right, dear boy," Beauty said, taking Tashgan's arm. "Let us go back to the feast. Your bride can join us as soon as she is able."

Tashgan nodded. "Fix her face before she comes down again," he ordered Lythande. Beauty dragged him out of the room, and Velvet sagged back down onto the bed.

"I see what you meant, Eirthe," she sighed, "when you told me to think of a way to explain the change in my appearance to him and wished me luck. There isn't a way, is there?"

"I've known him for over ten years and I can't think of one," Eirthe admitted. "Lythande?"

"I'm afraid his view of other people does tend to be superficial," Lythande agreed.

"That's a no, isn't it?" Velvet's smile was weak. "Well, if it's what my husband wants, I'll have to do it— especially since he can still set aside the marriage if he decides to."

"What?" Eirthe said.

"A marriage has to be consummated to be valid,"

Lythande explained. "Until that happens, it can be annulled quite easily."

"Especially after my lady-in-waiting tried to kill his champion," Velvet said wryly. "Today has been quite a day, and I still have tonight to endure."

"Tashgan did say that his wedding day would be long remembered," Lythande remarked.

"I don't think *I'll* ever forget it," Velvet said. "I've never seen an illusion contest like that. I'm still trying to figure out how Lady Beauty managed to kill Mirwen— not that I'm complaining. But surely Mirwen knew that the illusion of fire can't kill, so why did it kill her?"

"Because it wasn't an illusion," Lythande said.

"Of course it was an illusion," Velvet said, puzzled. "That's the whole point of the contest. You're not trying to tell me that Tashgan and I were in two places at the same time and that the unicorn and all the other animals were real."

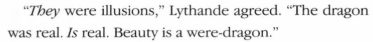

"*They* were illusions," Lythande agreed. "The dragon was real. *Is* real. Beauty is a were-dragon."

"Beauty is a were-dragon." Velvet was moving past shock into numb acceptance.

"Yes, but don't let on that you know," Eirthe said. "Just be very polite to her and make certain that you always listen to her music with proper appreciation."

"She is a wonderful musician," Velvet said.

"A few extra centuries of practice don't hurt," Lythande said.

"A were-dragon," Velvet repeated, shaking her head. "In a way that's a relief. I was afraid that Tashgan preferred her to me and was going to have the marriage annulled so he could marry her. But I guess that's silly."

"I think he wants human heirs," Lythande pointed out. "And besides, I don't think Beauty would agree to marry him. He's just a temporary diversion to her. She remarked to me at dinner that people come and go quickly, and from her viewpoint, they do."

"Yes," Velvet said, considering that matter. "After a few centuries, I guess we all look alike to her . . ." Her voice trailed off and she looked up at Lythande. "What she said about not having eaten any hearth-witches lately—she wasn't joking, was she?"

"I'm sure she hasn't eaten any lately," Lythande said, "but I do think she was joking. She has quite a sense of humor, and it's rather peculiar. But she's certainly pragmatic enough to realize that Tashgan needs a human wife, so as long as you don't antagonize her, you don't need to worry about her. She'll probably play the part of a doting aunt to your children."

"My children," Velvet sighed. "The point of this whole marriage. But I had hope that, if I had to marry, I would get a husband who could at least learn to like me as a person."

"Give Tashgan some time," Eirthe said consolingly. "He's not always as bad as he was today."

"But first we need to change her appearance so that

he'll look at her long enough to get a chance to know her," Lythande pointed out. "Go get the figure candles you made, please."

Eirthe nodded and hurried from the room.

"Maybe he'll get to like me in time," Velvet said wistfully. "He seemed to think the little girl was cute, and she took after me."

"I think he will," Lythande said reassuringly. "He's a bit on the shallow side, but he has a good heart."

"I hope you are right."

"So, Princess," Lythande asked, "is it your wish that I restore your appearance to what it was under Mirwen's spell?"

"Yes," Velvet said with resignation. "At least I don't have to look at myself. I only have to remember that what people see when they look at me isn't real and that their opinions of me are false."

"Only their initial impressions," Lythande reminded

her. "You *are* still the same person, and once they have known you for even a short while, that will still be what counts."

"Now that I'm married, what I look like doesn't matter much—as long as my husband likes the way I look. It's just too bad that he prefers the illusion."

"Your job is to consummate the marriage, be crowned beside him in three days' time, and bear children," Lythande pointed out. "The illusion spell is only a means to that end. And remember, Tashgan thinks the illusion is real."

"He does?"

"He doesn't know much about magic," Lythande explained, "and he thinks of beauty as a natural state. He thinks that Lady Mirwen cast a spell to change your appearance as she died."

"She died almost instantly, and she didn't see it coming," Velvet pointed out. "And she was thinking of something else at the time."

"Tashgan is not a deep thinker."

"Or even a shallow one," Eirthe said, returning with the candles. "Here you are, Lythande. I wasn't sure which you needed, and I wanted to keep them under my eyes, so I brought them all." She opened the boxes and set them out on the table.

"Set Tashgan aside for the minute," Lythande said. "We don't need him."

Eirthe carefully reboxed the Tashgan candle. "We'll need it for the feast. But we don't need Mirwen," Eirthe shoved the spider candle back into its box and handed it to Velvet. "Here you are. Do what you like with it."

The two versions of Velvet sat side-by-side on the table facing Lythande. Lythande dragged a chair behind them and waved Velvet into it. The salamanders arrayed themselves behind Velvet, near the ceiling, except for Alnath, who went to join Eirthe at the side of the room.

"Eirthe, Alnath, would you guard the door, please,"

Lythande requested. "I don't want to be disturbed while I'm working."

Eirthe nodded, and she and Alnath left the room, closing the door behind them.

Lythande looked at the pale and nervous princess. "Try to relax, Velvet. This isn't going to hurt, and if you don't look in a mirror, you'll never know the difference." She kindled mage fire to light the candle that showed Velvet's true appearance.

Velvet started crying as the wax began to melt. "I'll know," she sobbed. "Even without a mirror, I'll remember every time I look into my husband's eyes."

"Try not to remember," Lythande advised, watching wax tears run down the face of the candle and slide down the folds of its dress. "You are the only one who will be hurt by remembering."

She heard the echo of Eirthe's voice: *Velvet both benefits and is harmed by it.*

Velvet cried the entire time it took the candle to burn down, but stopped as soon as it was consumed. Now all that remained was the candle of the Velvet that Tashgan preferred and the living princess to match it.

"Will I always look like that now?" Velvet asked.

"Yes," Lythande replied. "Try to think of this as a wedding gift and make the most of it."

"It's funny," Velvet said. "I never wanted beauty—I always thought brains were more important."

"I think so, too," Lythande said, "but now you have both."

Velvet smiled weakly. On her new face, it looked radiant. "Thank you, Lord Magician."

Eirthe and Alnath came back into the room. "All done?" Eirthe asked brightly.

"You know perfectly well we are," Lythande said, "or you wouldn't have come in." She glanced up. "I supposed the salamanders told you."

"Of course." Eirthe nodded to the salamanders near

the ceiling. One of them detached itself from the group and moved to hover beside Velvet's right shoulder. "This is Caldon," Eirthe said. "He wants to stay with you, Princess. Will you accept him as a wedding gift?"

Velvet turned her head and smiled at the salamander. "Greetings, Caldon. I'm glad of your company." She turned back to the candlemaker. "Thank you, Eirthe. Now I won't feel quite so alone here."

Eirthe packed up the remaining candle. "I'm glad you like him. Not everyone deals well with salamanders."

Lythande quietly added an extra degree of resistance to burns to the spells on Velvet's skin as Velvet reached out to stroke Caldon with a tentative finger. Then she turned her hand over, and he hovered in the palm of her hand.

Velvet stood, moving Caldon to a position beside her right shoulder. "It's time to go back to the wedding-feast," she said resolutely. "I have a husband to charm."

Two nights later Lythande and Beauty were together in the hall packing up their lutes after another evening of musical duels. "I shall miss this," Lythande admitted. "I truly enjoy playing with you." She took a deep breath and asked the question which had been with her ever since Beauty's arrival. "Are you leaving tomorrow?"

Beauty raised her eyebrows. "And miss dear Tashgan's coronation?" Once again Lythande saw the were-dragon's "I know what you're thinking" smile. "Dear boy, I plan to stay at *least* another week."